THE TRUE SON

A STORY OF THE UNREMEMBERED KING

VANESSA MACLAREN-WRAY

*For my husband, my sons, my brothers, and my dad:
all different, all true.*

ACKNOWLEDGMENTS

My critique partners helped hone this little story: Drew Hoskins, Megan "Verb" Kargher, Chris Harget, Dennis Venturoni, and Taimur Ali Ahmed. Their advice was invaluable in making this yarn stand alone while also supporting the books it's tied to.

I should also acknowledge the unwitting participation of the instructors of the United Academy of Martial Arts, who let me observe and learn while they guided students to grow in their skills and develop both mental and physical discipline through forms, study, and sparring.

THE TRUE SON

Y OU ASKED ABOUT THAT SCAR, as if it's the only one I
have. As if I'm the only man walking around with
scars. As if it's proof of the rumor that I killed him.

Listen.

Foster-son to the king is a job with a long, uncertain
apprenticeship. Demands are high, but so's the reward
— for the family handing over their kid.

For most apprenticeships, the family pays up front
and reaps rewards later. For the king's potential
successors, the government pays at surrender. The thing
is, while the king may have a true-son who's technically
first in line, there's no guarantee the matriarchy will be
satisfied with that candidate. The king is supposed to
choose fosters who are smart enough to take all the
required education, tough enough to make a plausible
leader, and afflicted with the kind of heart that will put

the country's needs before his own. Every one of those boys is trained up as if he's going to step into those boots one day; once in fosterage, they're lost to their parents. Given you start as a little kid, by the time you wash out or get passed over for investiture, you're not much good for your family's operations — most end up working for the government in the end.

Which is why the payment's generous.

One thing about that: it widens the field of candidates. You might get ambitious rock-heads like Gorton, pruned from an oversized family of overeducated toffs. Or you might get a hammer-dragging kid from the manufacturing sector of Jeskaryan, a smith's son who never saw a written word in his life, but whose grief-stricken widowed father needed cash for a fresh start as a shaman.

Ya. That one's me. Corren, son of Orkast, last foster-son of Yutek.

There were six of us, once they closed that door behind me. We learned to call the king Father and his true-son (Yutek-en, that is) Brother, though day by day it became clear to each of us that Yutek-en was a monster. He didn't see other people as anything other than tools or targets. Good old Yutek didn't deserve such a creature as his only true-child; I'm not sure how much he knew of his son's brutal treatment of servants and animals ... and his foster-brothers. The staff worked hard to keep him unaware of it, though I expect the matriarchy received reports. Whether they believed those reports, that's another story.

You can't get around the fact that they did invest him, laid upon him their approval as Yutek's successor. What would this country have done if he hadn't died before his accession? The Council of Elders would have had to have him killed. If he'd revealed himself after taking the kingship, there wouldn't have been another way. The chief Elder would have called up the guard commander and said, *Take care of this.*

And Magaran would say, *Yes, ma'am.* Then he'd look over his captains and pick one and say, *Take a troop and clean up the trash in the council chamber.*

Likely he'd have picked me. I decided early on that my path forward was the Guard — the combination of army, police force, and personal protection agency that keeps Jeska safe from invaders, brigands, and insurrection. Soon as Yutek put his stamp of approval on it, I signed up for under-guards. We got to spar with wooden swords, learn basic hand-to-hand, and generally smash each other up good for a couple of hours every day. It meant I had to work harder the rest of the time — studying history, memorizing rituals, listening to Father's lectures on Ruling Jeska the Yutek Way — but it was worth every minute.

Because Yutek-en *had* to be in the guards.

It wasn't optional for him, because ultimately, the king is commander-in-chief of the Guard. Besides, hurting people was a natural part of guard practice and Yutek-en's personal unnatural hobby. Most of the other kids in under-guards learned to stay out of his reach. Me, not so much.

Thing is, my brother Tymon — my truest foster-brother, the one who taught me the ropes of the job, who gave me his trust and loyalty and friendship — was Yutek-en's favorite target. Unlike the dogs, servants, or random citizens singled out for the true-son's favors,

Tymon didn't fight back or cry or beg for mercy. He wouldn't give Yutek-en the satisfaction he most needed.

My favorite bouts in under-guards were when Captain Magaran would put me and my enemy together. I'd let my anger take over, and there wasn't anything Yutek-en could do against it. Coated in sweat and sand, he'd retire to his cushy rooms upstairs in the king's house to nurse his bruises and plot revenge. I was a kid. I was foolish. I meant for him to shift his attention to me, but it didn't work. Life for Tymon only got worse.

I rose through the under-guards fast, but so did Yutek-en. He might have been a monster in his spare time, but he was a skilled fighter. I hate to say it, but sparring with him made me a better guardsman. There are brigands who owe their deaths to moves I worked at in order to defeat my brother's abuser.

When they married Yutek-en off to that unfortunate lady from up North, we knew his investiture was imminent. Marriage for a prospective king is never based on attraction. Though even an impromptu arranged marriage can work out well for both parties, that's not the point. The system suited Yutek-en, who hadn't done much to ingratiate himself with any Jeskaryan women. He had his circle of cronies, pals who enjoyed helping him torture his underlings, but none of them had partnered up, either. It should have been a sign to Yutek that there was something wrong with his son, but they say parental sight is flawed.

Mine isn't. My kids are perfect in every way.

Well. Cal's impulsive. And will lay you out flat if you offend him. Stevvin will be sneaky when he should be direct. I'm pretty sure Affram cheats at games, but Stevvin says he doesn't. Smacks of conspiracy. Delia's perfect, but I attribute that to her mother, who is the same way.

I suppose that's one more thing I learned from Yutek: to be aware of my own thoughts.

•   •   •

Sure enough, the day after the marriage, Yutek-en's wife marched down the hall to demand a private apartment for herself — and the officials scheduled his investiture ceremony.

Tymon didn't show up for lessons that morning. He'd never missed. Not even once. I searched the king's house from top to bottom, and found him squeezed into a cupboard under a stairway, reviewing the texts we'd been supposed to cover with the tutor earlier. It was midsummer, sweltering hot, but he'd pulled on a long-sleeved jacket and dragged his trouser legs right down to the tops of his boots.

I haven't mentioned this, but off-duty, Tymon preferred going barefoot.

I didn't ask. I didn't make him show me. Lately, Yutek-en had been experimenting with the effect of heated blades on skin.

"Come on."

I took him by the hand and led him down to the practice yard, round the barracks, and to the cold pool. I made him take his boots off, but didn't make him strip. I'd learned that burns tend to stick to clothes. If there were cuts, pulling off the fabric would rip off any clotted blood.

Best to soak first.

No one was around, so I left him to go steal a uniform out of the laundry. He was already much taller than me, more filled-out. Anyone seeing us together would have guessed Tymon to be the guardsman-in-training and me the protected little brother. Anyone who didn't know us, that is.

We got him cleaned up, and I stole some salves from the medic's trunk, and we slipped back up to the king's house, to our closet of a room. He was exhausted.

"Sleep," I told him. "I'll check on you after guard practice, all right?"

He didn't say anything, just rolled over to face the wall. Salve bleeding through the fabric made dark spots on the clean shirt. I tore my eyes away and pulled on my own uniform.

•   •   •

To my surprise, Yutek-en showed up in the practice yard.

"Aren't you supposed to be getting invested?" I asked him.

"Soon enough. Figured I'd get a light workout in."

He twirled the blade he'd grabbed for the day's session. Sunlight flickered up and down the steel.

We'd long graduated from wooden-sword drills. Dulled blades won't kill you, but you need the threat of injury to get serious about learning your defensive moves — even when it's still mostly grinding through forms.

I snagged one of my favorites from the practice bin. "Ya. Me, too. Good day to work up a sweat."

I could feel the shadows of my anger roiling at the back of my mind. I tried to keep them crowded back, to leave my vision clear.

"Good enough. Let's wait until everyone gets here."

Yutek-en liked being the center of attention. When you're being invested, you have to stand out in the plaza, in public, with all your clothes off, and the elders — a pack of nosy old ladies — look you over. If they ever tried to invest Tymon, there'd be a lot of questions about his scars, but it seemed to me, even then, that Tymon would have been a much better choice than Yutek-en. Me, they'd never get *me* to stand up there showing off my undersized figure.

If he needed to stall, I needed to keep in motion. I moved off a bit and ran through a series of forms. I had a set I'd worked out that combined some of the showier moves: Bear Crunch, Rolling Log, River Twist. Sometimes we'd put together performances for Yutek to admire, running routines in unison, letting individuals show off a little.

I pushed myself, treated the practice as a statement for Yutek-en. *I'm gonna crunch you like this. Then I'm gonna roll you under, like that. And I'll twist your arm off, you overconfident thug!*

When I rocked through the conclusion, spraying sand high overhead as I skidded under the arm of my imagined attacker, eviscerating him as I passed, a scattering of applause echoed from the walls of the practice yard.

My fellow senior trainees had arrived, all of us not-quite-troopers, ready to sign our contracts as soon as Magaran would let us. I lowered the blade and gave them all a salute, which was returned in varying styles from hilarious to deadly serious. Don't get me wrong, the jokesters by and large were good guys, some destined to be commanders one day. It takes a certain kind of skill to know the difference between a formal gesture and a celebratory one.

Then a deep, familiar voice filled the air above the yard. "Well done!"

Yutek descended the steps to the yard, plain-looking in the soft brown shirt and trousers he wore on days he'd be overloaded with ceremonial robes later on. His bodyguard followed: six men in their formal uniforms.

So the investiture really was happening. This afternoon.

Was today's sparring to become part of the event?

Well, I wouldn't be laying down my sword and yielding to Yutek-en just because our father was in attendance.

I pulled a towel off the stack under the side-shelter and tidied myself up. Without needing to think about it, I checked the blade for nicks and verified the bonding held at the tip and the edge hadn't developed any sharpness from being dragged through the sand.

A group of staff members scuttled under the canopy and arranged chairs hurriedly as Yutek and his entourage approached. I saluted instead of bowing, which when I was younger would get me a rub on the head, but now earned me a respectful nod and a swift salute back.

I loved Yutek almost as much as I loved my true-father. I hoped he'd live forever, see Yutek-en's bones scattered before his, and pass the kingship to Tymon.

With the king in attendance, Magaran made the session more formal than usual. He had us line up, run through some stock forms, do a few cheers to get the old man's smile to shine, and pair off for a few quick hand-to-hand bouts.

He didn't pair me with Yutek-en, which annoyed me. The other guy, a little taller, with a nice, straight, unbroken nose, took the brunt of it.

Which is to say, I smashed his nose.

Sorry, Durse.

Yutek-en was equally disappointed. His partner had to be carried off the sand. If it had been an ordinary session, Magaran would have had words for him. For me, too. But not today, with Yutek watching.

"If the two of you are going to be like that, bash each other," the captain growled at us.

When he set up the blade demos, then, he put us together. We both wanted to get right out there, but he made us wait.

I think he was trying to instill discipline, but it only made matters worse. Yutek-en kept giving me the side-eye, his lips twitching that way he had when he was up to something nefarious. That look meant, *Lose, or else I'll get Tymon after this.*

I bounced on my toes to keep the blood flowing and shrugged my shoulders to keep from tightening up after that earlier performance of mine. What I meant by that was, *Lose? To you? You losing loser?* I'd protect Tymon. Somehow. I had ideas I hadn't tried yet.

By the time the captain called us out to perform, we were both of us out of our minds. For Yutek-en, that meant he'd forgotten our father was there, forgotten all the ways he kept his nature hidden, forgotten everything except how he'd put me on the ground, shame me in front of Magaran and my future comrades-in-arms. For me, that meant my vision had narrowed down to a dark-rimmed tunnel revealing only the target of the moment; my entire body had become a device, like something made by a mad smith, a thing with one purpose: to destroy Yutek-en.

Of course, it was two teenagers with practice swords, surrounded by actual guardsmen, on a practice field.

Nothing was really going to happen.

Yutek-en struck first. He always did that. Then he'd pull back and yammer insults, as if a rational circling attack was somehow cowardly.

I knew better than to listen to him. I watched for the moment he'd glance at one of his buddies, hovering there at the edge of the field, to catch an appreciative smile. Then I dodged in and thwacked him good, right on his sword arm, at the elbow joint.

He yelped as his hand went numb and the sword dove towards the sand.

I expected him to catch the hilt with his left hand, in his usual way, but instead he slapped his thigh with his free hand and a knife appeared. He slashed quickly, before I could react, and nearly caught me sleeping.

I dodged back, called out to the captain, "Sir?"

We weren't supposed to be using two-blade technique in free sparring, because there's no such thing as a dulled knife. I kept my eyes on both blades in play: the bright slicer in Yutek-en's left and the sparring sword he was picking up off the sand. If I turned to appeal directly to the referees, I'd be out of the match before I could say anything. I had to trust the captain to make a judgment call.

Out-bladed, I circled, considered ways I could take him, even with the doubled advantage — I had to keep account of his longer reach. Could Magaran not see the knife? Or did he need to defer to Yutek?

"Point to Corren!" came from one of the referees.

Yutek-en spat and smiled, running his tongue over the edges of his teeth. He meant to goad me into attacking. I entertained a brief fantasy of hammering his chin, letting him bite off the end of his tongue.

I circled, edging closer, but not too close.

He spun the knife, rotated it to an upthrust position, and took an advance posture, sword tight to his body, ready to slam outwards.

I circled, but reset, ready to block.

"Two blades!" Magaran shouted.

It didn't take more to send my free hand to my own leg, to withdraw my sweet little fighting knife. As I did that, I whirled into a spinning attack, while Yutek-en was still readying himself. He wasn't prepared to block, so he didn't have enough power to push me off.

So I kicked him in the shin.

He yelped again. I swear flames shot out of his eyeballs.

That ended the preliminaries. We went for it, then, both of us.

Attack, block, riposte, break off, the occasional punch or kick for variety. My style involved a lot of spins and rolls — good for a smallish guy. He went more for leaps and wide swings of the sword backed by feints and parries with the knife.

I gave him back, move for move. We couldn't help cutting each other some with the knives. All a part of the game — and the reason we weren't generally allowed to engage this way, apart from drills. Then again, Yutek-en never liked games. He only liked winning. Moment by moment, he grew angrier. His eyes went tight and narrow, the sneering smile became a grimace, lips parted only enough to let him breathe. Every time he cut me, I took in a good breath and held my silence. Every time I cut him, he cried out. How could he ever go into battle like that?

He covered for it with words. If we were in a clinch, he'd whisper something of what he meant to do to Tymon next. If we were standing separate, he'd shout something for the audience to enjoy — call me a motherless peasant, a lackwit laborer. Some reference to my class and status. At one point, he dodged a knife-strike only to get his knee thwacked good and hard, because he was only watching the one blade.

"Shaman's son!" he shrieked at me. "Dishonorable scum!" Shamans being celibate means they only have children if they've broken their vows.

He couldn't hurt me that way. Orkast sold me off when I was six, before he became a shaman. I was the price of his apprenticeship.

I broke my silence, and barked out a laugh. Orkast had been an armorer first, and taught me early how to swing a hammer. I twirled my blade, set it in a grasp you never use with a sword, and brought it down on Yutek-en's head.

Well, he dodged. The dulled blade hammered into his shoulder, sending him to his knees.

Another "Point for Corren!"

Referees had been calling points the whole time, though neither of us kept count. Most of his points came from knife-work — that was the long reach talking. Or did he mean to win by waiting for me to lose too much blood? The cuts weren't that deep. I was too fast for him. Most of mine were blade taps: knee, shoulder, one on his butt. That one fired up his anger. Back in the wooden-sword days, it would have counted as a death-blow. We'd often played that you tapped out the limbs first, and if you'd been tapped you couldn't use that limb. He seemed oddly hesitant with the blade. Maybe that first blow to the elbow tendon hurt more than usual.

Not that I didn't work with my knife. I loved that knife. Orkast had brought it for me, from one of his shaman wanderings. He claimed it came from another world, but that it came from him was good enough for me. I sliced vents in Yutek-en's shirt until it flapped like a dancer's costume, parried his knife, ran the hilts together and spat on his blade, turned my hand and punched him in the chest with the hilt.

That feels like being stabbed in the heart. We all know that move.

Yutek-en immediately tried it on me, but I was too fast, sliding under his arm exactly as I'd closed out my form sequence. It being a sparring match, not battle, I didn't eviscerate him, but caught his arm as I skidded, and dragged him to the ground. He lay on his back, chest heaving, and the dusty sand fell out of the air and into his face.

"Point to Corren! Match the next!"

I waited for him to get up. That's what you do, sparring. It's not war. It's a contest.

A contest I was going to win.

The round turned to feints and dodges on both sides. The shift in his approach threw me for a few seconds. I left him an opening for a tag, and he failed to even attempt the strike. Was he tiring? I pressed for advantage, but he held his own, matched me glide for glide. It was more like we were acting out a routine than fighting. He even mimicked my knife-work, cut slashes in my shirt. No points, only style.

Finally, he pulled a new move.

I admit it. He surprised me. Must have been practicing with his henchmen, because I heard a chorus of laughs rise from that corner of the yard when he did it.

Here's the stunt part: he tipped his knife up, grasping it with only his thumb, then latched his fingers onto one of the dangling strips he'd sliced in my shirt, and yanked, hard, throwing me into an unplanned spin. It could have been only that, a trick to make me trip over my own feet, earn him a point by falling on my face.

But there was more to come. As I started to spin, he raised his sword. The flash of the sun along its length tore my attention away from the knife, and I saw what was coming, in the instant before I'd spun to leave my back exposed.

Thing is, sunlight on a properly-edged blade is a thing of beauty. It's like the sun's fire has laid itself along the cutting line, a perfect slice of molten fury.

Practice swords don't do that.

A tag is a painful, bruising blow; done right, it can knock the wind out of you. But it won't drive the threads of your uniform jacket into your flesh. slice a gash from your shoulder to your hip, and spew blood onto the sand.

Yutek-en followed me down as I fell, crouched to put his face next to mine, and snarled, "You won't be taking over my father's job, gutter-walker."

The knife flashed as he flicked it back to a proper grip, ready to finish me off — but Magaran could move fast when he wanted to. Yutek-en yelped, and his knife hissed into the sand in front of my face.

I tried to get up. Moving made it feel like he was cutting into me again, but I didn't care. "You're dead," I growled. "Dead, dead, dead."

He'd been reaching for the knife, but backed off. Even his shadow moved away. I think someone was dragging him back. I got one knee partway under me, but my arms couldn't push my body up. Magaran was shouting at me, "Stop, stop, the match is over, Corren!"

"No," I said. "It's not over. It's never over with him."

But I yielded to the captain, let him push me back flat on the sand, while someone ran for a medic and someone else shoved towels into the wound that was making a mess of our beautiful practice yard.

"Everything's ruined, Captain," I told Magaran. "What'll we do when they make him king?"

•　　•　　•

I missed the investiture. That was the only good part of the day. I didn't have to stand there in the sun and watch Yutek-en get the king's mark burned into his skin. I didn't have to go to the party afterwards and look happy about anything. The medics took the better part of an hour to sew me up, and wrapped bandages around me until my whole torso was nothing but wrappings. I'd have been decent at the celebrations without a shirt, but I wouldn't have been coherent. They fed me half a jug of cider and sent me to bed.

Good stuff, cider. Goes to your head when you aren't used to it.

Deep in the dark nothingness, long hours into Yutek-en's first day as heir-in-fact, Tymon nudged me out of my stupor. "Corren, Corren, I've got to get out of here. The party's winding down, and you know — you know —"

I knew.

I'd failed him that afternoon. Yutek-en meant to kill me, but I survived. He might very well kill Tymon, just to prove he could, to send me a message. I couldn't risk it, no matter how much I wanted Tymon at my side.

"Help me up."

He was gentle, careful to avoid the injury. So someone had told him everything. No wonder he was terrified. Sitting up made me a little dizzy, but not much. I could think, that was what counted. What I had in mind was going to hurt, but it was the only way.

I pulled on an extra shirt over the one I'd been sleeping in, dragged my uniform jacket over that, then wrapped a belt tight, to keep everything in place.

I tried not to think about my back.

At least I couldn't see it.

"Come on."

We made it to the kitchens without anyone interfering with us. There were a fair number of partiers lolling in the hallways, but they didn't care much about two youngsters enjoying a late-night stroll. The staff seemed to have quit for the night, though they'd left stacks of trays unscraped and unwashed. The major-domo'd be on somebody's case tomorrow.

I got us to where the little door opened to the sluiceway, the garbage chute, the dishwater dump.

"What're we gonna throw away, Corren?"

"Us."

His eyes went wide and round. Took me back to that first day, when we were six and seven, meeting for the first time at the fosters' dorm. Then he grinned. And I remembered how none of what happened back then troubled him, because we were together.

"It's dangerous," I warned him.

The grin stayed. "*He* wouldn't dare try this."

"No, he wouldn't." Imagine Yutek-en sliding down a garbage chute. "Listen. I've scoped it out. None of the drops are too bad, but it's dark, so stay low, don't let yourself bounce up by the edge."

"Right. I get it."

I opened the hatch. It was only a little smelly. The last use must have been washwater. Tymon put a hand on my shoulder — the one away from my wound — and pressed softly.

"I'll go first," he said. "I'm bigger, I can keep you from sliding too fast."

I could have argued, but he was right. So we went. Tymon first, me after. I managed to tug the sluice door closed before the drop took me. Had to slide on my back for the first stretch, until we were out of the pipe and into the open gutter. Tymon dragged himself to a stop at the brink of the second drop, to wait and help me get to a solid sitting position.

That saved me. If I'd slid the whole way on my back, I'd have done worse than pull a few stitches out. Despite the pain leaking through, it was the most fun I ever had, sailing down that slide, with just my brother and the Jeskan moon for company, all of us — even the moon — fighting to keep from laughing out loud at our daring and the sheer thrill of the ride.

•   •   •

I took him to Runner's House. I'd thought of taking him to the shamans, to my true-father, but Orkast was likely off on a hunt for secret passages to the Other World, and besides, I really didn't like the shamans. A lot of people don't like the couriers' guild; they have some weird ways, but it's all centered on the family, the family that is Runner's House. I knew they'd like Tymon, his perseverance and good humor, and he had the right makings to do well for them, with his educated brain and his long, tireless legs. For his part, my brother needed to be surrounded by people who cared about him. From then on, he wouldn't have to make do with only me.

He cried when I left him. I made all my cheerful, happy, encouraging faces, and so did the adults in that House, and the little kids, and the people our age.

On the long slow walk back up the hill to the fortress gate, I was probably crying, too. I passed a couple of late-night wanderers in the market sector, and they looked at me funny. The gate guard acted strange, too. I told him I'd gotten drunk, which was true, and that I felt sick, which wasn't, but could stand in for feeling like I was going to drop dead right there and make this a perfect day for Yutek-en.

He sent for help, and gave me some more cider while we waited, so that was good. Turns out more cider makes you feel better. Why hadn't anyone told me that before?

•　　•　　•

I left it for the next afternoon, to go tell Yutek. He was sitting at his desk in the king's apartment, nursing a drink of something that smelled terrible. He made me sit across from him and asked me how I was doing. I told him I'd messed up my stitches some, but the doctor said if I didn't care too much about the scar it'd be all right. He laughed a little, then rubbed his forehead and sipped some more of his drink.

"I wager the doctor didn't go easy on cleaning up the mess."

"No, sir."

He grimaced and downed another dose of what was probably a hangover remedy.

I was about to add to his headaches. "Tymon's gone, sir."

"What?"

"He had to leave, sir. I helped him. Sorry." I didn't know what else I should say.

My back was starting to hurt again. I couldn't sit straight, and couldn't bend over, either.

"We're down to you, then, Corren." Yutek had his eyes trained on me. I could tell, even though I kept mine focused on the table between us. "I started with six fosters, and here I've only got one who hasn't washed out or resigned."

"But you don't need us, now, do you, sir?"

"Don't I?" He had his true-son all set up to succeed him. I had a sudden sickening thought. Would Yutek-en kill his own father?

He might.

Well, he might try. I'd have to keep an eye on him. "I'm not going anywhere, sir."

He chuckled, and that made me look up. "Glad to hear it, son." He waved his fingers in that way he had, to tell me to look him in the eyes. I did that for him, not to be obedient, but to show I was listening. "The Council of Elders can change their minds any time, Corren. The succession isn't a sure thing until they carry it out." His gaze drifted down to the bandages peeking from the edges of my shirt. "They get reports. The matriarchy knows everything."

He seemed to expect an answer. "Yes, sir." That one's always safe.

He grunted. "Father."

"Sir?"

He kept silent, looked at me steadily, gestured at me, *Come on,* that military code that also means *Pay attention*.

"Yes, Father," I said.

"Keep that in mind. Don't let anyone tell you otherwise. Not anyone." He picked up his pen and slid a stack of paperwork closer, waving me off.

"All right then, Father."

It's a job, being the king's foster-son. It's a job you learn day by day, battle by battle. I'd no idea how far I'd go, but I wasn't going to run from it. Not then. Not ever.

AUTHOR'S NOTE

For more about Corren and Tymon, and less about Yutek-en (one hopes), spin the wheel forward in time and follow their adult lives in the novel *Shadows of Insurrection*. You'll see how Corren's career in the Guard plays out, watch Tymon's role as a runner turn both their lives in strange directions, and find out if Yutek-en does anything at all good for the nation of Jeska.

And as if that's not enough … war is coming to Jeska, and the brothers will face new changes as they fight to save their country from those who would destroy it—in the second half of the duology, *Flames of Attrition*.

ABOUT THE AUTHOR

Vanessa MacLaren-Wray writes science fiction and fantasy exploring the challenges of communication and attachment in a diverse, complex universe. She hosts regular online open mics for the California Writers Club and acts as a guest host for the podcast *Small Publishing in a Big Universe*. She is also an active member of the Science Fiction and Fantasy Writers of America (SFWA).

As an energy systems engineer, she has analyzed electric power systems, studied climate-safe technology, and written extensively on energy issues. The oddball robots she builds out of kids' toys and stray parts do not seek to destroy humans — instead, they brew tea and play music. Vanessa lives in farm country, where fields of strawberries and artichokes hold the developers at bay. When not arguing with her cats, she works on new stories, her email journal *Messages from the Oort Cloud*, and her website, *Cometary Tales*. Find all her connections at *linktr.ee/Vanessa_MacLarenWray*.

ALSO IN THIS SERIES

SHADOWS OF INSURRECTION

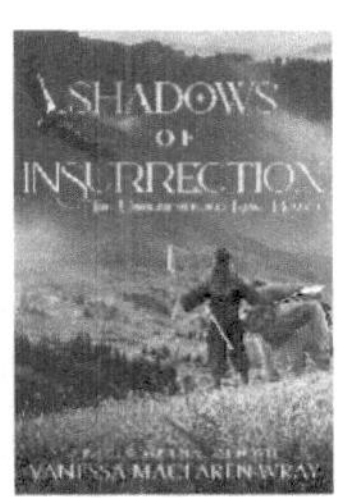

BOOK ONE OF THE UNREMEMBERED KING

by Vanessa MacLaren-Wray

Once in a generation, the matriarchs of Jeska choose a new king to manage the government and command the Guard—protecting Jeskans from crime, invaders, and insurgency.

FLAMES OF ATTRITION

BOOK TWO OF THE UNREMEMBERED KING

by Vanessa MacLaren-Wray

Once in a generation, the matriarchs of Jeska choose a new king to manage the government and command the Guard—protecting Jeskans from crime, invaders, and insurgency.

ALL THAT WAS ASKED

A PATCHWORK UNIVERSE NOVEL

by Vanessa MacLaren-Wray

Varayla Ansegwe — perpetual student, aspiring poet, and scion of the (allegedly) criminal Syndicate — didn't volunteer for this alternate-world exploration mission, and the rest of the crew have had it up to here with this pampered noof.

Available in
hardcover, trade paperback, digital, and audio editions from
Water Dragon Publishing
waterdragonpublishing.com

ALSO BY THE AUTHOR

COKE MACHINE

FROM THE "TRUCK STOP AT THE CENTER OF THE GALAXY"
by Vanessa MacLaren-Wray

Every truck stop needs a coke machine.

PARRISH BLUE

by Vanessa MacLaren-Wray

Sallie never expected to discover a world she'd forgotten how to imagine.

THE SMUGGLERS

FROM THE "TRUCK STOP AT THE CENTER OF THE GALAXY"
by Vanessa MacLaren-Wray

Attachment is everything.

Available in
hardcover, trade paperback, and digital editions from
Water Dragon Publishing
waterdragonpublishing.com